Flying Tigers

A Boy's Adventure

RICK LAVENDER

Cover by Bruce MacPherson Design

Front cover: collage includes the Liberty Foundation's P-40 Warhawk
Back cover: includes U.S. Department of Defense photograph (P-40 in flight)

To my wife and children.

CONTENTS

ACKNOWLEDGMENTS

This book is a daydream put to print. Yet even some daydreams involve work. This one certainly did, for many people. My sincere appreciation goes to all who helped.

My wife and children patiently steered the book through many revisions, doubling as editors and trusted advisers.

My parents and my mother-in-law gave welcomed encouragement and confidence. Good friends Jeff Gill and the Williams family volunteered as proofreaders, helping derail more than a few errors.

A special thanks to Bruce MacPherson, of Bruce MacPherson Design in Bishop, Georgia. Bruce spun ideas and photographs into a striking cover.

Don Brooks, chief executive officer of the Liberty Foundation, and Ray Fowler, the foundation's chief pilot, graciously allowed access to the P-40 featured on the front cover. The Liberty Foundation (*www.libertyfoundation.org*) restores and uses vintage warplanes to honor veterans and raise awareness of aviation history.

Father and son pilots Ray and Winn Fletcher reviewed the flying passages and provided key insights and corrections. Ray is a retired Air Force B-52 command pilot who worked for 30 years with the Georgia Department of Transportation's Bureau of Aeronautics, now called Aviation Programs. Winn is a member of Experimental Aircraft Association 611, based in Gainesville, Georgia.

Through all, I am grateful to God, who gave the ability to wonder, the desire to write and the freedom to dream.

❂ Chapter 1 ❂

June 1974

Tommy Coleman stared across the field of corn. The green rows shimmered in the summer heat. Long lines of plants curved together, reaching like fingers toward dark trees in the distance. Except near the middle of the field.

There, the waist-high plants gave way to a long, thin stretch of grass. Probably longer than a football field, Tommy thought, guessing at the length. A building sat near one end of the grassy opening. Tommy squinted, trying to see details. The building was colored the creosote brown of old telephone poles. It was wide, with a tin roof and two tall doors on the side facing Tommy. That much he could tell. Nothing else.

A breeze stirred the corn. Tommy felt sweat on his forehead. "Sure is hot," he said. His voice sounded loud. Although he was standing in the shade of a large pecan tree, the air felt as if it had been heated in an oven. Where the shade ended, sunshine baked the yard of thin bahiagrass and bare patches of sand.

Even the gnats won't go out there, Tommy thought, swatting at the small insects hovering around his face.

This was his grandfather's place. Grandpa Buck lived in a small brick house on a slight hill overlooking fields and a dirt road in southern Georgia. The house and yard and three pecan trees and a metal grain bin poked up like an island in a sea of corn. Grandpa and Memaw, Tommy's grandmother, had lived here for 40 years. Before that, the house and the fields had been home to Memaw's family for more than a century.

When Memaw died, Grandpa never thought of moving. Now Tommy was moving in, if only for the summer.

He liked the idea. His mother would be there. On weekdays, she would attend college in a city an hour away, taking classes to become an elementary school teacher. His dad would continue to work out of their home on the other side of the state. Tommy's parents planned to sell that house and starting in the fall build another at the edge of Grandpa's farm.

To Tommy, who had turned 12 that spring, the change sounded like an adventure. He hated leaving his friends and starting the seventh grade at a new school. Yet, if he really thought hard, he had to admit that life had not been easy at his former school. Besides, he liked to explore and fish. Grandpa's farm seemed to offer plenty of room for those things. Woods and ponds and creeks lay beyond the corn.

But Tommy realized as he looked across the expanse of green that although he and his parents had sometimes visited the farm on Thanksgiving, he had spent most of that time playing with his cousins and, as his mom liked to say, eating like a pig. In all of that, he had not seen much of the farm.

Like that barn or whatever it was, Tommy thought. And that long field of grass in the corn. He could not remember seeing either of them.

Grandpa Buck was built like his house. At least it seemed that way to Tommy. His grandfather was not too tall, as plain as the orange bricks and white wooden trim on the outside of the house, and as sturdy as the heart-of-pine frame underneath. He had a soft laugh and light green eyes behind gold-rimmed glasses. The back of his neck and hands were leathery and tanned red-brown from working outdoors.

His name was Buck Tillman. He had been born and raised in south Georgia. He and Memaw married and moved into the house on the hill in 1933. A few years later, after the crops had been harvested, Grandpa joined the U.S. Army Air Corps. He told Memaw he wanted to be a pilot. However, the Air Corps saw the red-faced farmer with less-than-perfect eyesight as an airplane mechanic.

By 1940, he had trained at schools and military bases in the states. When the Japanese bombed Pearl Harbor in Hawaii in December 1941, Grandpa was soon in the thick of World War II, serving at island airfields across the Pacific Ocean. As he later told Tommy, "I spent the war cleaning bullets, sand and salt out of warbirds."

After the fighting ended, Grandpa returned to his coal-haired wife and three young children. He began work with the Postal Service and spent nearly a lifetime delivering mail, farming and helping Memaw raise Tommy's mother, her brother Charlie and her sister Ruth.

Grandpa also did something else: He taught himself to fly.

He had received some training in the Army Air Corps, a forerunner of the U.S. Air Force. After the war, Grandpa corresponded with his World War II pilot friends and studied an Army flight manual until the pages were rubbed thin at the corners and some had pulled loose from the binder. For $400, he bought a double-winged Stearman trainer plane the military no longer needed. Grandpa rigged the Stearman to spray crops with chemicals and for 20 years he worked weekday evenings and some Saturdays as a part-time crop duster.

A large black-and-white photograph still hanging in his living room captured that part of Grandpa's life. Escaping the summer heat outside, Tommy had wandered into the room. It was crowded with furniture. A wooden rocker, an orange recliner and a lumpy cloth sofa all faced a television placed between two potted plants.

Tommy was drawn to the photograph. He knew it so well he could close his eyes and still see the details.

In the image, a younger Grandpa grinned and leaned against the plane. Painted in fat letters on the aircraft's side was the company name – Buck's Aerial Applications – and the company motto, "Dust or Bust."

Tommy grinned, too.

"Those were the days," his grandfather said, walking up behind him.

"I bet," Tommy said quietly. "When was the last time you flew?"

"That plane? Oh, I sold it a long time ago," Grandpa said.

"Do you still want to fly?" Tommy asked.

Grandpa hesitated. "Well, I do like to fly," he said.

Tommy remembered the building and stretch of grass in the cornfield. "Grandpa, there is a barn in the field behind the house and something that looks like a skinny football field, but it's much longer than a football field. What are they for?"

Grandpa started to answer but stopped as the kitchen door swung open. Tommy's mother pushed the door shut behind her. The slender woman with wavy brown hair swept into the small kitchen and dropped an armload of books onto the table with a loud "Whew!" She tossed her purse into a chair and smiled at her father and son.

"Hi!" she said. "What are you two up to?"

Grandpa seemed unable to answer. He glanced at Tommy. "We're, uh, talking. About storage."

"Storage?" Tommy and his mother said at the same time.

"Yes," Grandpa said, his voice firmer. He turned back to his grandson. "That's what you were asking about, Tommy. The building and storage. That's what is in there. Tools and ... and other things."

"Oh," Tommy said as if he understood, although he really didn't.

His mother looked at Tommy then Grandpa. "Glad I could help you clear that up," she said.

"Me, too," Grandpa replied, sounding grouchy. "Now, I've got a garden that needs hoeing and no excuse not to be doing it. I'll see you two at supper!"

He stomped past Tommy and his mother and out of the house.

✪ Chapter 2 ✪

The Barn

The garden's neat rows of sweet corn, peas, string beans, peppers, tomatoes, okra and potatoes ran between the cornfield and the dirt road. Tommy followed his grandfather outside. He planned to offer to help and of course ask again about the building and the field. Thinking about how he would do both, he almost did not see the red pickup truck parked in the yard next to the grain bin.

The silver, circular bin used for storing corn and other grains stood 10 feet tall and had a cone-shaped top. A boy sat in the truck on the driver's side, one leg dangling from the open door.

"Hello," said Tommy, forgetting Grandpa and the garden.

"Hi," the boy said. He swung around to look at Tommy.

They eyed each other. Tommy decided the boy looked about his age, but he was thinner, with a long, straight nose and hair the color of corn shucks poking from under a red Massey Ferguson Tractors cap.

"I'm Tommy," Tommy offered.

"My name's Sam – Sam Roberts."

"Oh, Mom told me about you," Tommy remembered. "You and your dad farm here, don't you?"

"Yep," Sam answered. He glanced toward the grain bin. The clangs of someone hammering echoed from inside it. "That's why we're fixing your granddaddy's grain bin."

Tommy felt his cheeks turn warm in embarrassment.

"Well, of course, I can see that. I mean, I can hear it," he stammered.

If Sam noticed Tommy blushing, he did not mention it. Instead, he looked straight at Tommy and asked, "Has your granddad shown you the back barn?"

"The what?"

Sam nodded toward the cornfield. "That barn out there."

Tommy knew instantly what he meant. "Uh, no, he hasn't."

Sam sounded surprised. "Really? Everybody knows."

Tommy started to ask, "Knows what?" but the clanging had stopped and Sam's dad was calling.

"Sam, bring me the big ball-peen hammer! It's in the toolbox. And come in here and help me hold this piece in place."

"Yes, sir," Sam said. He slid from the seat and began searching through a tool box in the bed of the truck.

"Well, looks like you've got work to do," Tommy said. "I'd better go. But good to meet you. Maybe I'll see you around."

"Sure. We live just down the road," Sam said. Head down in the toolbox, he added, "Everybody knows."

Tommy did not get a chance to talk with his grandfather until after breakfast the next morning. His mother had left for class, gulping down her water, kissing him on the cheek, and staring at him briefly before smiling and saying what a wonderful day she knew he would have.

The rising sun sliced bright yellow paths across the kitchen as Grandpa and Tommy carried dishes to the sink. This is as good a time as any, Tommy thought. Clearing his throat, he began, "Grandpa, what you said about that building in the field yesterday, it didn't really make sense to me."

Grandpa stopped, dishes in hand. "Probably that's because I did a poor job of telling you," he said slowly.

"Maybe seeing is the best way of making sense."

Grandpa put the dishes in the sink, walked to a drawer at the end of the counter and began to rummage through it. The shallow drawer was crammed with things: scissors, screwdrivers, bread-bag twist ties, screws, nails and half-used rolls of electrical tape.

"You can never have too much electrical tape," Grandpa mumbled. He fished a metal ring with two keys from the jumble. "Let's go," he said.

They walked in silence through the back yard and around a large shed where Grandpa kept his garden tools and lawnmower. Behind the shed, Tommy was surprised to see a path just wide enough for a car or pickup truck. The path led through the half-grown corn. The shed and the plants mostly hid it from view.

From here, Tommy could see the barn and the opening in the cornfield. The path pointed toward them.

Grandpa led the way, following tire ruts pressed into the sandy soil. "We could drive, but might as well get some exercise," he said.

They soon reached the barn. It was twice the size of Grandpa's house. Double doors that reached to the roof and opened on rollers took up most of the front. There was a normal-sized door beside them, but no windows. Nearby, a rusty fuel tank perched on metal feet in knee-high weeds.

The barn bordered the grassy stretch. Tommy saw that it was much larger than he had originally thought, about half as wide as a football field and six times as long. The grass looked as if it had been mowed. Corn surrounded it. Dragonflies flitted silently across the grass. Blue sky stretched like a dome overhead. A stack of hay bales stood in front of a dirt mound at the far end of the field.

Grandpa unlocked the smaller door. "Ready to see inside?"

"Sure," Tommy said.

However, when he stepped through the door and his eyes adjusted from the sunny brightness outside to the shadowy coolness inside, Tommy was not sure if he could even speak. When he did, it was only one word, said in a whisper:

"Wow."

Grandpa stood, arms folded and smiling. Behind him was an airplane. Yet, not just any airplane; a huge one with a long thick nose, a massive propeller with black blades tipped in yellow and a gaping mouth with pointed white teeth. The plane was olive green and sat back on its tail, as if aimed upward. Fat tires as tall as Tommy's knees supported stubby wings that were silvery white underneath. The cockpit was nearly as long as the width of the wings. On the side of the plane was a large white star in a blue circle.

The airplane towered over Tommy. "Wow," he whispered again.

Grandpa chuckled. "Do you have any idea what kind of aircraft this is?"

Tommy tried to remember what he had read about airplanes. The star on the side looked like a U.S. Air Force marking, maybe an old one. There was something, too, about the shark-like mouth painted on the nose. Tommy suddenly remembered where he had seen the image before.

"There were fighter planes in World War II that had that ... that mouth on the front!" he said. "Is that what this is?"

"That's what this is," Grandpa agreed, sounding pleased. He patted the wing. "It's a P-40 Warhawk. A World War II fighter, one of the first and most used. One that could take a real beating and keep flying. I worked on many of these in the Southwest Pacific."

Tommy couldn't believe what his grandfather was saying. A World War II fighter plane. In his grandfather's barn! In the middle of a cornfield! And he was touching it.

"Can I touch it?" he asked, realizing with a start that he was running a hand along the wing.

"Touch it all you want," Grandpa said as he walked to the front of the barn.

The plane's green metal skin felt cool and smooth between lines of small round rivets that looked like stitching. Tommy noticed that the metal changed to stiff fabric on flaps along the back of the wing. He followed the wing, carefully ducked under it and came up beside the mouth.

Painted in a snarl with rows of sharp teeth and a red tongue, the mouth curved across the bottom of the nose. A white eye with a black pupil stared unblinking above the teeth. With the spinner of the propeller providing the pointed nose, the mouth and eye gave the big green plane a face. A war face, thought Tommy.

He stepped back and something poked him between the shoulders. Turning around, he saw that he had bumped into one of three thick, silver pipes protruding from the wing. Gun barrels!

A loud rumbling made Tommy jerk back around. Grandpa was rolling open the doors.

"Grandpa," Tommy asked as sunlight spilled into the barn, "does it fly?"

Grandpa smiled again. "Does it ever!" he said.

❂ Chapter 3 ❂

A Bit of History

With the big wooden doors open, Grandpa and Tommy pushed the plane off the barn's concrete floor and onto the grass. Tommy was amazed they could move it.

"I use my riding lawnmower if I don't have somebody to help," Grandpa said, grunting as he pushed. "OK, that's far enough. You stand right here and hold this."

Grandpa handed Tommy a radio headset. He pulled himself to a sitting position on the left wing where it joined the fuselage, turned and stood up. Grabbing the edge of the open cockpit, he swung one leg over the side and into the back. Grandpa steadied himself before climbing in the rest of the way. He slipped on a pair of goggles.

"OK, Tommy," he said, concentrating on something inside the plane then glancing back at his grandson. "Now you get to hear a bit of history.

"Clear prop!" he yelled and grinned at Tommy.

The P-40's engine whirred rhythmically, sounding like a car trying to crank in winter. The propeller blades began to trace slow, looping circles. Drops of fluid spurted from underneath the plane. The tips of the wings shook. Tommy held his breath.

The engine coughed, sputtered, then caught again. It roared to life. A blast of sound and wind made Tommy stumble backward. The propeller spun into a black blur. Thick, oily exhaust washed over him. Through the stench and the roar he heard Grandpa calling, "Are you gonna stand there all day?"

"Sir?" Tommy shouted back.

"Are you coming or not?"

Tommy realized Grandpa was wearing a radio headset. Tommy looked down at the one in his hands. "This is for me?" he said to himself.

Grandpa waved toward the front of the cockpit. "Crawl up on the wing like I did. Sit here!" he yelled over the rumbling engine.

Tommy felt his pulse thumping as he scrambled onto the wing. A black, foot-wide strip as rough as sandpaper ran the width of the wing. "Stand on that while you get in and you won't slip!" Grandpa instructed.

Tommy reached for the cockpit, looked in the front and saw a seat padded with a boat cushion. He pulled himself over the side. The cockpit smelled like canvas. Grandpa tapped his shoulder and motioned for Tommy to put on the headset, pointing to a plug-in jack for it. Tommy heard crackling, then Grandpa's voice.

"The radio headset is voice-activated," Grandpa said. "I rigged it up myself. Just speak and I'll hear you.

"Now, sit back in the seat and strap yourself in. I put new safety belts in. They buckle like a car seat belt."

Tommy fumbled with the straps. He finally got them untwisted and fastened.

"Close your cockpit canopy next. It's separate from mine," Grandpa said. "Use the hand-crank on the side. See it?"

"I do," Tommy answered, spotting the small handle. As he turned it, the canopy slid forward over his head and sealed shut. The barrier of thick glass muffled the sound of the engine, but only slightly.

Tommy gazed in wonder. The black panel in front of him

had clusters of round gauges with white markings, and rows of silver switches. At the top edge of the panel was a small square of glass. Levers and knobs lined the sides of the cockpit. At his feet, Tommy noticed metal pedals, one for each foot. Sticking out of the floor in the center was a slender pole with a black rubber top. It looked like the gear shift in Grandpa's truck.

He twisted around. His grandfather was intently looking at something – another control panel, Tommy guessed. Turning back to the front of the canopy, Tommy could see only the plane's nose, the hazy black of the spinning propeller and blue sky. The upward tilt of the P-40 made it impossible to see the ground directly ahead.

"Are you all locked in?" Grandpa radioed.

"Yes, sir."

"There's a pair of goggles hanging on that lever to your left. Put them on."

"Got 'em."

"OK," said Grandpa. "Here goes."

Tommy felt the vibration of the plane increase. The sound of the engine rose and fell. "Just checking things out," Grandpa said. "We're about ready."

The engine growled louder. This time, it did not let up. The P-40 began rolling toward the grass field, swerving from side to side. "I can't see the ground in front of me," Grandpa said. "So I swing back and forth to see where I'm going and make sure I don't run over anything. Like my lawnmower."

When they reached the edge of the grass, the plane stopped. Tommy now knew the field was a runway. Above it he saw wisps of white clouds in an endless sky. A sky he would soon reach? The thought sent a shiver through him.

The P-40 started rolling again. It picked up speed quickly. The cockpit rattled and shook. Corn stalks flashed past.

Suddenly Tommy was looking straight ahead, not up. The tail of the P-40 had lifted.

Then Tommy felt the rest of the plane leave the runway.

One moment they were bouncing along the grass, clouds of dust boiling behind them. The next moment they were gliding smoothly upward. Clearing the edge of the corn and the line of trees, Grandpa retracted the landing gear and swung the P-40 back over the barn and house. Buildings, roads and fields below grew smaller as the plane climbed.

The radio crackled again. "How are you doing up there?" Grandpa asked.

Tommy stared out of the side of the cockpit. Grandpa's house looked no larger than a matchbox. The landscape stretched out in blocks of crops and clumps of woods. Fences and roads framed fields and forests. Ponds – more ponds than Tommy could remember – looked like blue mirrors. Tommy could even see the peanut warehouse and the water tower in town 10 miles away.

He had never flown before. He could only compare it to the feeling he had when the Ferris wheel at the Jaycees fair stopped with his chair at the top. The bench seat rocked slightly as he looked down on the other rides and the carnival tents and trailers. The experience left him tingling and a little woozy.

Now, instead of stopping, Tommy kept sailing upward.

"It's like a dream!" he said into the headset's mouthpiece.

"I knew you'd like it," Grandpa said. "We'll take her around for a quick tour and set her back down."

Grandpa flew over Franklin Christian Church, the church he and Memaw helped start. Next came thick woods threaded with creeks. The dark green mass reached unbroken to the horizon. "That is Warrior Swamp," Grandpa said.

Along the eastern side of the swamp, the woods ended at

fields of row crops – corn, soybeans and peanuts. Beside one house, a boy looked up and waved wildly. Minutes later, Tommy saw Grandpa's barn and the grass runway in the field. The runway looked small. Too small.

Tommy looked away, noticing again the stubby barrels in the wings.

"Grandpa," he said, "those are guns on the wings, aren't they?"

"Yep. 50-caliber machine guns. Three on each side."

The plane was approaching the runway and gradually dropping toward it.

"Do they still shoot?" Tommy asked.

His grandfather did not answer. The runway drew closer. Finally, Grandpa spoke.

"Hang on!" he said.

Tommy could do nothing but hang on as Grandpa tipped the plane's nose down. Wide-eyed, Tommy grabbed the sides of his seat with both hands. The P-40 plunged toward the cornfield. Tommy could see only green rising to meet him. He wanted to scream but couldn't. He could not even move his head. The acceleration pressed him into his seat and squeezed the air from his chest.

Just above the field, Grandpa pulled the aircraft out of the dive and aimed it down the runway. The hay bales at the other end rushed toward them.

Tommy heard the clatter of guns firing. He glanced at the right wing and saw the machine gun barrels puff flames. He looked ahead. Furrows of smoke zipped toward the field. Explosions of sand danced across the grass. Then the bullets hit the hay. Straw blew out the back of the bales and dirt sprayed as the 50-caliber rounds plowed into the earthen hill behind the bales.

Grandpa swept over the target and pulled the roaring plane

up and to the left. Tommy felt his spirit soar with it.

"Waaahooooo!" he yelled long and loud.

Over his headset, he heard Grandpa yelling, too.

✪ Chapter 4 ✪

Warbird

T hat night, Grandpa explained how and why he bought the P-40 Warhawk. First, though, Tommy learned that his mother knew about the plane and about Grandpa's plan to take him flying.

"So how was it?" she asked. Her eyes studied his face.

"It's hard to describe, Mom," Tommy said. "Scary, fun, crazy. Like the first day of school and the wildest fair ride in the world all in one."

His mother smiled. "That's wonderful. Your father will want to hear all about it when he calls. He really wanted to be here but he couldn't because of work."

"Yeah," Tommy said. "Maybe by the time he calls I can think of a better way to describe it."

At his grandfather's suggestion, Tommy had invited Sam to join them for supper. Grandpa promised to tell all about what he called "the warbird" after they finished eating.

The boys worked their way through two helpings each of fried chicken, baked sweet potatoes, field peas and thin pieces of hoecake, a round, salty cornbread Tommy's mother cooked in a cast iron skillet. As she washed the dishes, Grandpa moved to his rocking chair in the living room.

"Sam already knows some of this story," he started. "He and his dad and brother have helped me keep the plane up. They have even helped me keep watch over it."

"Keep watch over it?" Tommy asked. "Why?"

Grandpa began rocking. "Let's just say there are plenty of people interested in that warbird."

Sam looked solemn. "Everybody knows," he said.

Grandpa and Sam looked at each other, as if sharing some thought in silence. "Maybe too many," Grandpa agreed. He turned to Tommy.

Grandpa said that after Memaw died of cancer, a World War II buddy offered to sell him the P-40. The friend was a former pilot who wanted to restore the plane but never finished it. Grandpa and Memaw had sold a small farm she inherited in the north Georgia mountains, thinking they would use the extra income for her hospital bills.

They did not need it. Memaw's death came quicker than expected.

Grandpa gave some of the money to add Sunday school rooms and a heated baptismal pool at Franklin Christian Church. "I also set aside a good part for your mom and dad, and your uncles and aunts," Grandpa said to Tommy.

He paused, staring at the wall. "Sitting around with more grief than I wanted and more money then I cared for, this plane became available at a bargain price. Something inside me said it was an OK thing to do. I figured it was an investment. I'd keep the warbird awhile, fix it up and one day sell it for a profit.

"That's still my plan," Grandpa said. He wiped his eyes with the back of his hand.

He and Sam's father had picked up the plane at a warehouse in Florida. They partially disassembled the Warhawk, loaded it on a flatbed trailer and wrapped it in tarps. "We hauled it straight up Interstate 75," Grandpa said. "I already had the runway ready."

Mom asked from the kitchen, "Isn't the landing strip in the same spot you used when you were crop dusting?"

"Yes, it is," Grandpa answered. "Fact is, flying the warbird is somewhat like a crop duster. It's a tail-dragger. The third wheel is under the tail instead of the nose. That makes it more challenging to fly in some ways, but it also makes it a whole lot easier to take off and land on grass.

"Of course, the Warhawk has tons more power than a crop duster. It also has more instruments, and more age. Everything is older. Me included."

Tommy and Sam laughed.

"I fly it a few times a week. Short trips only," Grandpa added.

"Was it used in World War II?" Tommy asked.

Grandpa explained that the P-40 was America's first full-scale fighter plane in the war, particularly in the Southwest Pacific, North Africa and China. Built by the Curtiss-Wright company, the P-40 was rugged, faster than many enemy fighters and more maneuverable than some of them at low altitudes. "Some people don't think too highly of it," he said. "But I did. I still do."

He said that in China, the American Volunteer Group and its commander, Lieutenant General Claire Chennault, made the P-40 famous. Flying P-40s with China's air force at the start of the war, the American Volunteer Group was credited with destroying nearly 300 enemy aircraft in the air and on the ground, while losing fewer than 15 pilots on combat missions. ("Some say the AVG didn't down quite that many planes, but either way it was a lot more than they lost," Grandpa said.) The Americans also bombed bridges and supply lines. They earned their nickname the Flying Tigers defending Burma and China against the Japanese. The crews had painted shark mouths on the P-40s, copying the idea from a picture of a British plane with a similar design.

Grandpa chuckled. "Chennault said he had no idea how

the name Flying Tigers came from a bunch of shark-nosed P-40s. Somebody said officials in the states had already decided they would call the volunteers Flying Tigers. So I guess both the shark's mouth and the tiger nickname stuck.

"Anyway," Grandpa said, "many other nations also used the Curtiss P-40 – Britain, Russia, Australia, even New Zealand. They called different versions the Tomahawk or the Kittyhawk. The Flying Tigers used Tomahawks. For later models of the plane, the U.S. stuck with the name Warhawk."

"I like Warhawk," Sam said.

"Me, too," Grandpa said. "But the Warhawk's days serving our nation were numbered. Faster, better fighter planes like the P-38 Lightning and the P-51 Mustang came along in World War II and replaced the P-40, and rightly so. They could manhandle the enemy better."

His chair rocked gently as he talked. "So while other countries with smaller air forces kept using P-40s, the U.S. moved on. One of the last versions of the P-40 is the one I have. The fighter is a one-seater, but mine is a trainer. That's why it has two seats and two sets of controls."

Grandpa stopped. "I never did answer your question, did I, Tommy?"

Tommy smiled. "No, sir."

"Well, this plane never flew in combat," Grandpa said. "Still, there are not too many P-40s left in the world today. A plane like this draws lots of attention."

"Which is why people try to get you to sell it to them," Sam said.

"Yep," Grandpa replied. "And for now I'm not interested. Of course, some people don't like 'no' for an answer.

"But that," he said, looking at Sam, "is a story for another day."

✪ Chapter 5 ✪

Sam's Secret

Afterward, Tommy walked with Sam part of the way to Sam's house. Sam lived less than a half-mile from Grandpa.

"Watch for rattlesnakes!" Tommy's mother warned before they left.

It was late and the sky was bright with stars and the light of a half-moon. The dirt road looked like a silver ribbon in the moonlight. Sand and pebbles crunched underfoot. Crickets sang in the ditches along the road.

"Well, now you know," Sam said. "At least, you know most of it. There are other things only a few people know."

The last part of Sam's comment sounded strange to Tommy. "What do you mean?" he asked.

"There's more that your granddad didn't tell you," Sam said. "But maybe he will."

Tommy did not reply. Seeing the Warhawk, taking his first flight and hearing his grandfather's story had left him tired – peaceful, but tired.

The two boys walked slowly. A Chuck-will's-widow called, sounding out its name over and over. Fireflies flashed in the trees and brush in front of Sam's house, tiny points of light blinking on and off against the black. Cows mooed in a pasture far away. The deep thrumming of bullfrogs called from a pond. The warm night smelled of earth and corn.

Sam spoke again. "Of course, I got things to worry about."

This time Tommy answered from the quiet inside him. "Like what?"

"I don't know if I should say."

Tommy started to say that was OK, Sam could tell him when he was ready. But Sam was already talking.

"It's my brother," he said. "He works as a deputy with the sheriff's department. And he's onto something. Something big, I think."

Sam seemed to struggle for more words. "It may be drugs. Somebody's flying them in. Using crop dusters. Even Dad seems worried."

Tommy stopped walking. Sam continued a few more steps before he noticed he was alone. He looked back.

"Sam," Tommy said, "what in the world are you talking about?"

It took Sam a while to explain. He said his brother, Ben, might have uncovered a local trade in illegal drugs. According to bits of information Sam had pieced together, a pilot would pick up the drugs somewhere along the Gulf of Mexico and fly them to south Georgia. They were loaded into cars and trucks and carried to cities farther north, such as Atlanta. "A crop duster can haul things other than chemicals," Sam said.

"Why bring them here in the first place?" Tommy asked.

"Look around," Sam said. Tommy did. Besides the fireflies, the only lights he could see were those at Grandpa's house and at Sam's.

Sam continued. "Lots of farms and woods. Few people. And who looks twice around here when a crop duster flies past?

"There have been rumors. But lately I overheard Dad and my brother talking more. Something is up."

The boys had reached halfway. Both stopped. Tommy was

not sure what to say. "Is there any way I can help?" he asked.

"Probably not," Sam said. Head down, he scratched in the sand with one shoe. "Thanks anyway. You'll be at church tomorrow." It was more of a statement than a question.

"I guess so," Tommy said. He turned back toward Grandpa's. "See you tomorrow."

Tommy reached the house just as his mother was opening the back door to call for him. "Your father is on the phone," she said.

Tommy hurried inside and picked up the phone. It was good to hear his dad's voice. Tommy realized how much he missed him. They were close, even if his father's work as a salesman for a company that made fertilizer kept him on the road most days and nights during the week.

Tommy told him all about the P-40 and what it felt like to fly. However, it was what his father said just before they hung up that Tommy remembered most.

"So, son, you're going to learn a little about flying."

"What did you say, Dad?" Tommy asked.

"I said you will be learning more about flying," his father repeated. "Has Grandpa talked with you about lessons?"

"No, sir," Tommy said. He felt his excitement rising again, almost like when he climbed into the Warhawk.

He thought he heard his father sigh. "I have probably gotten ahead of your granddad," his father said. "If he hasn't talked with you about it yet, he will. Soon."

✪ Chapter 6 ✪

Sunday

Tommy intended to ask Grandpa about the flying lessons the next day. Yet, that was Sunday and Tommy soon realized his questions would have to wait until after the morning service at Franklin Christian Church. Before the service, Grandpa talked little.

At least going to church will be interesting, Tommy decided.

He did not think of himself or his parents as religious. They had sometimes attended a big church with white columns and a long, green lawn in the city where they used to live. Franklin Christian Church was different. The building was only slightly bigger than Grandpa's house and shaped like a shoebox. It sat in a grove of pine trees beside Warrior Swamp. Members parked among the trees, which occasionally dropped pine cones on the cars, as if to remind the owners the area had once been all forest. Grandpa said another congregation had planted the church 40 years ago. He meant formed. Considering the setting, Tommy thought that planted was a good description.

Grandpa and Memaw had helped found the church and build the building. The sanctuary with rows of shiny wooden pews that smelled of lemon-scented wood polish had not changed much over the years. But members had installed a window air-conditioner. It replaced the hand-held cardboard fans that a local funeral home used to supply each Sunday.

On this summer morning, the air-conditioner rattled bravely in a losing battle with the rising temperature outside.

Tommy paid more attention to Grandpa. His grandfather sang hymns in a deep, gravelly voice that was out of tune. He sometimes greeted the pastor's preaching with a loud "Amen!" It made Tommy jump the first time he heard it. His grandfather also listened intently to the sermon, flipping through his worn Bible as the pastor cited verses. Tommy glimpsed his mother watching Grandpa, too.

Even Sam seemed serious about church. As the congregation sang the chorus "on Christ the solid rock I stand," Tommy glanced at Sam, sitting three rows away. Sam was singing with gusto. Sounds like Grandpa, Tommy thought. Sam caught his eye and smiled wide.

After church came Sunday dinner, which was dominated by talk about when it might rain and when the Atlanta Braves might win. The odds of either happening seemed hopeless to a bored 12-year-old boy.

Next, Grandpa moved to his rocking chair. He held the latest issue of the weekly newspaper in one hand. "Sunday is a day of rest," he declared. Within minutes, his eyes closed, his head tilted back and the newspaper slipped into his lap. He was asleep.

Tommy turned to his mom. She had replaced the plates and leftovers on the kitchen table with textbooks and a yellow notepad.

"Mom, I wanted to talk to Grandpa and now he's asleep," Tommy complained. "Is there anything around here to do?"

His mother looked up from her books. "Sorry, but I am not your entertainment organizer. You think of something."

"Can I walk down to Sam's?" Tommy asked.

"That's fine," his mother said. "Just be home in time for the evening service."

Sam will be as miserable as I am, Tommy thought. Instead, he found his friend turning the knobs on a CB radio attached under the dashboard of his father's truck. Sam had told him that CB stood for citizens band, a short-distance radio that farmers and some law enforcement officers in the area used. The radio popped and hissed like a pot of boiling water.

Tommy peered in. "Hey, Sam. What are you trying ..."

"Shhhhh!" Sam said. "I'm trying to hear something."

Sam twisted a knob. The static stopped. A man's voice spoke hurriedly.

"This is Yellow Dog. I'm coming home. Have dinner ready. Over."

A deeper voice answered. "10-4. Will do. Route clear."

The static started again.

"Well, that was really interesting," Tommy said. "Some guy who calls himself a dog is coming home to eat. What else can you pick up on that radio? The loudspeaker at Dairy Queen?"

Sam fiddled with the knobs. "I think those were the people flying in drugs!" he whispered fiercely. "The ones I told you about. They speak in some kind of code. Dad's radio can sometimes pick up their contact because Ben had a special crystal installed to cover more radio frequencies."

"Oh," Tommy said.

Neither boy saw Sam's brother walk up. Ben was not in uniform, but he still looked like a sheriff's deputy. He stood 6 feet tall, with square shoulders, ice-blue eyes and a buzz haircut that would make the U.S. Marines proud.

Tommy had met Ben at church that morning. He had not looked as stern then.

"Hello, Tommy," Ben said in a flat voice. "And hello to you, Sam. Why are you using Dad's radio?"

Sam quickly switched off the radio. "I ... I was just listening to something," he stumbled.

"Listening to what?" Ben pressed.

"Just something," Sam said. He stared at the floorboard.

"Sam," said Ben, his tone more gentle, "there are things I'm involved in that you don't need to be. They are not safe for you. I appreciate your interest. But you have to stay out of this.

"You have to," Ben repeated.

✪ Chapter 7 ✪

Time to Fly

Grandpa's voice reverberated through the house. "Tommy! Rise and shine. It's time to fly!"

Tommy threw off the covers and glanced at his alarm clock – 7 a.m.! He began frantically pulling on his pants and shirt. "I'm coming, Grandpa!" he yelled.

Outside, the morning sky was milky blue. Crows wheeled over the tree line beyond the cornfield, cawing and diving at a red-tailed hawk in a tall pine. Tommy and Grandpa checked over the P-40, wheeled it out of the barn and got in. Minutes later, they were thundering over the cornfield. Tommy grinned in excitement. The crows scattered.

"We'll go for a short flight," Grandpa said over the radio. "Take time to look around the cockpit. Ask any questions you want."

"Yes, sir," Tommy answered. Then he began asking. "What are the pedals for?"

"Mainly they move the rudder on the tail fin," Grandpa said. "The rudder controls the direction of the plane's nose."

"So the rudder turns the plane?"

"Well, you turn or bank using the rudder and the ailerons, those flaps at the back edge of the wings, near the end. The ailerons on each wing are connected. They control how you steer with the wings."

Tommy looked out at the wings. "What changes the ailaon ... the airleenos ... I mean, what changes those flaps?"

"The control stick," Grandpa said. "You move the stick and press the rudder pedal at the same time to turn. One aileron goes down, increasing the lift of that wing. That means it rises. The other aileron goes up, making that wing go down. Applying the rudder keeps the back end of the plane from skidding sideways. Watch this."

The plane began to veer left. Tommy saw the metal pole sticking from the floor between his feet tilt the same way. The left pedal pushed in slightly.

"See the control stick and the pedal moving?" Grandpa asked. "I'm doing that. Your stick does the same thing as the one I'm using. Because this P-40 is for training it can be flown from either my seat or yours.

"But always remember this about flying a plane," Grandpa said. "Learn right, do it right and don't take chances. You got that?"

"Yes, sir."

"Would you like to try it?"

"Yes, sir!" Tommy almost shouted. He could not see Grandpa grab his headset.

"You don't have to yell, son," his grandfather said. "I'm not deaf yet. OK, so hold the control stick handle with your right hand. Be gentle. Don't push it fast one way or the other. Try to keep it straight.

"And whatever you do, don't go messing around with the trigger on the front of the handle. That's for plugging holes in hay bales!"

Tommy curled his fingers around the black rubber grip made for a hand bigger than his. The stick vibrated with the energy of the plane. For Tommy, the sound of the engine and the blue sky above and green fields below faded away. He focused on the feel of the control stick. He did not know how long he had control. He only knew that it seemed too soon when he heard Grandpa say, "I'll take it back now."

After they had landed and pushed the plane back into the barn, Grandpa leaned against a wooden desk near the doorway. "Well, Tommy, do you want to learn to fly?"

Tommy nodded. "I think I'd like to."

"It's not easy," Grandpa said. "But you can do it. You're smart enough, and big enough. You're also tall for your age. That helps. It will take work, though. Lots of work."

Twisting around, he grabbed a thick book on the desk. He handed the book to Tommy.

Tommy read the cover: "Pilot Training Manual for the P-40." The year 1943 was printed in thick black type in the bottom right corner.

"Learning to fly begins with studying – hard," his grandfather said, watching Tommy's face.

Tommy nodded again. Grandpa smiled. "OK," he said, "now help me put this warbird to bed."

They dusted the plane with soft rags. Grandpa checked for loose rivets and other signs of wear. Tommy stopped to admire the brightly colored shark's mouth. A line of exhaust pipes above the mouth looked like gills. The plane truly looked like a shark.

Grandpa noticed Tommy studying the design. "Not all P-40s had that face," he said. "But those that did made the aircraft one of the most recognizable used in World War II."

"Is that the reason people want to buy it?"

Grandpa paused before answering. "That popularity and the fact that it is now a very rare plane. Both drive the price up."

Tommy was not sure if he should ask more. As they left the barn, Grandpa turned off the lights and clicked another switch.

"Alarm system," he said in explanation. "Wired it myself.

That way I know if anyone enters this place without me."

"Grandpa," Tommy said, "how much is the Warhawk worth?"

Grandpa had already reached the path through the corn. "Considering the design and the fact that the plane is in such good shape," he said, "I'd guess a million dollars. Or more."

The figure of $1 million was on Tommy's mind two mornings later when a silver car pulled into his grandfather's driveway. Tommy and Sam were playing a basketball game of H-O-R-S-E, taking turns shooting at a rusty basketball rim they had nailed to the side of the backyard shed. Grandpa was hoeing in the garden.

Tommy heard the crunch of tires in the sandy driveway. In the garden, he saw his grandfather straighten, grip his hoe in both hands and walk toward the driveway. Grandpa's face was grim. He looks like he just saw a rattlesnake, Tommy thought.

"Uh-oh," Sam muttered.

"What's up?" Tommy asked.

Sam ignored the question. "Come on," he said. "Let's get closer."

From the edge of the carport, they could see Grandpa talking to someone on the passenger side of the car. The window was down. Tommy glimpsed a broad-shouldered man with black hair and black sunglasses in the front seat. The glare of sunlight on the windshield hid the driver.

Tommy could hear only part of what Grandpa was saying. What he could hear, however, made one thing clear: His grandfather was mad.

"I told you I am not interested!" Grandpa said loudly, his voice carrying across the yard.

The man in sunglasses must have replied. He smiled, white teeth shining in a tan face. It did not look like a friendly smile to Tommy.

The man's response seemed to anger Grandpa more. Grandpa's voice rose further. "You got two options," he said, stepping back from the car. "Leave on your own or with my help!"

The man still smiled. Tommy saw his shoulders shrug. The car eased forward, curving back toward the road. As it went past the carport, the man with the sunglasses and the cold smile spotted Tommy and Sam. He nodded and said in a husky voice, "See you later, boys."

Grandpa marched back to the garden and began working furiously. His hoe rose and fell repeatedly, shearing weeds in small bursts of dirt.

Tommy could tell Grandpa did not want to talk. But Sam did.

"Those are the people who want to buy your granddad's plane," Sam said, picking up the basketball and tossing it to Tommy. "They have been bugging him for months.

"At first they sounded nice. After your granddad told them about 20 times he did not want to sell, they stopped sounding nice. That's what my dad told me."

"Where are they from?" Tommy asked. His shot slipped through the rim.

"I'm not sure," Sam said. "I think the car is rented. They have a different one every time they come. Dad thinks they drive down from Atlanta or somewhere."

Sam missed his follow-up shot.

"That's 'S,'" Tommy said, keeping score for him. "Why do they make Grandpa so mad?"

"'Not sure about that, either," Sam said. "Probably because they're so pushy."

Tommy rang a hook shot. "Grandpa is not one to push around."

"Everybody knows that," Sam agreed.

"By the way," he said as his shot bounced off the rim, "can you be quiet while I shoot? I have a hard time shooting and thinking."

"Everybody knows that, too," Tommy said. "That makes 'E' for you."

✪ Chapter 8 ✪

Dark Clouds

In Tommy's opinion, the following Saturday was close to perfect.

He and his father had gone fishing on Warrior Creek with Sam and his dad that morning. They first sprayed each other with insect repellent that smelled like orange peels. To reach the creek, they pushed through briars and cane stems so thick they sometimes had to crawl. They pointed their fishing poles behind them to avoid getting the tips broken or the line caught.

The tangled brush gradually gave way to tall trees in an open, shaded bottom land. Warrior Creek flowed through the hushed forest, winding unhurried over white sand and swirling around gnarled tree roots.

At every deep pool, the boys and their fathers swung hooks baited with crickets into the tea-colored water. As soon as one of the crickets sank out of sight, a bream grabbed it, yanking the cork under and sending the tight line tracing quick circles as the fish pulled against the pole.

Each bream that Sam considered big enough to eat went on a nylon stringer. The men and boys caught about 100 by mid-morning. They spent an hour that afternoon scaling and cleaning the short silver-green fish with bellies tinted rose, orange or yellow.

Tommy's mother and Sam's coated the bream with corn meal. Sam's father dropped them into a tall aluminum pot half-full of oil and heated over a metal burner, and fried them until they turned golden and crunchy.

Tommy and Sam ate until they were stuffed.

Tommy also considered the day special for two other reasons: His father had seen him fly and Sam had taken his first flight in the P-40.

"That was quite impressive," Dad said as Tommy climbed out of the cockpit. His father had watched from the runway, standing with Sam and his dad.

"You have to try it, Dad!" Tommy urged. "There's nothing like it."

"I'm sure you're right, son," his father said. "But your Grandpa and Mr. Roberts and I have been talking about sending somebody else up."

He paused. "Somebody a bit younger."

All of the men smiled at Sam. It took Sam a few seconds to understand why. "You mean I can, I mean, go in that?" he asked, looking at his dad and the P-40.

"You can if you want to," his father said. "I trust Mr. Tillman."

Grandpa took Sam for a spin over his house and buzzed the cornfield as the fathers and Tommy whooped and waved. After a bumpy landing, Sam scrambled out of the cockpit yelling to his father, thanking Grandpa and laughing.

Tommy smiled at the memory and slid farther down into a lawn chair. Sam's parents were talking with Grandpa in the house. Tommy's parents had gone home. Sam was somewhere, Tommy thought lazily. He had been up since dawn. The long day and big supper had left him drowsy.

The clouds of an evening thunderstorm slowly climbed the sky. Breezes carried the distant roll of thunder. Cicadas droned like small power saws in the pine trees. Katydids blended in their chattering hum.

Something else hummed. It even sputtered. Sam had switched on his dad's CB radio, Tommy realized.

He pushed himself out of the chair with a groan and walked to the truck.

"Hear anything?"

"Not yet," Sam said. "At least not on this thing"

Sam adjusted the dials as he talked. "I overheard Dad talking with Mom about this stuff again. He sounded worried about Ben. He also mentioned something about not being sure who all is involved."

"What do you mean?" Tommy asked.

"I guess there's big money in selling drugs," Sam said. "A lot of folks around here could use more money, or maybe they just want more. I heard Dad say that a guy in town may be involved. He's a crop-duster pilot. He also works at the grocery store, I think.

"The word is he sometimes uses his plane for flying in drugs. And get this, the plane is yellow!"

Tommy stared at Sam. "You think that's the person we heard call himself Yellow Dog on the radio?"

Sam nodded. "Easy money can make for a load of temptation, I figure. It can even turn neighbors into enemies, if you know what I mean."

Tommy thought he did.

When he and Grandpa drove home that evening, the storm had drawn closer. Slate-colored clouds billowed high into the sky before them. Veins of lightning laced the gray, followed by thunder that shook the air.

"Grandpa," Tommy said, "are you afraid those men who came by the house this week will try to steal the Warhawk?"

Grandpa looked at him. "I hope they won't, Tommy. Actually, I'm praying they won't. But, honestly, I just don't know."

As they got out of the car, the dark clouds hung over the house and fields. The air felt heavy and still, as if waiting.

Tommy heard the rain coming across the corn. The soft roar of millions of drops pounding into the plants and earth grew louder and louder. Then the wall of sound and water enveloped the small house on the hill.

❂ Chapter 9 ❂

August

"**H**old tight, Tommy! This is what they call a hammerhead!"

Tommy followed his grandfather's instructions, gripping his seat as Grandpa pulled the P-40 into a climb. It was the middle of August and Tommy had been taking flying lessons for two months. The hammerhead, however, was a new maneuver. And not a comfortable one, thought Tommy as he began to grow dizzy.

The Warhawk lost speed as it flew straight up, finally slowing almost to a stall. The plane balanced briefly on its tail, then rolled sideways and fell in a sickening drop along nearly the same path it had climbed. Tommy watched as the airspeed indicator topped 300 mph before Grandpa smoothly eased the plane out of the dive.

"That is an exaggerated version of a crop-duster move," Grandpa said through the headset. "It allowed us to make a tighter turn at the end of a field. In a showy way, of course."

"Did fighter pilots do that, too?" Tommy asked.

"Not in P-40s." Grandpa turned the P-40 toward Warrior Swamp. "This plane was not as agile as most of the fighters it faced. But it did have a higher top speed. It could also dive faster.

"For example, General Chennault taught his pilots with the American Volunteer Group to slash and dash. Attack, dive, then, if they needed to, outrun anybody who got on their tail.

"Still, the P-40 could turn good at high speed," Grandpa continued. "I have heard pilots talk about turning hard out of a dive and catching the enemy in their sights. These 50-caliber guns had a longer range than the firepower on some other planes."

Tommy peered through the gun sight. The rectangle of glass slanting toward him at the top of the control panel had a small ring with a dot in the center. Tommy had read in the flight manual about how to aim. Pilots framed targets in the ring-and-dot sight. Tommy imagined a silver enemy plane in front of the Warhawk. The plane twisted and swerved as it tried to escape him. It was no use.

Smoke from the P-40's tracer bullets streamed toward the fighter. The glowing rounds marked the path of the shots, just like when Grandpa had strafed the hay bales.

Grandpa's voice interrupted his daydream. "You want to try it?"

"Shooting?" Tommy asked.

"No," Grandpa said quickly. "I meant some of the maneuvers we just talked about. Diving and turning."

"Oh, sure," Tommy said.

He grasped the control stick more firmly to feel the movement he would soon try to copy. With his index finger, he gently touched the gun trigger on the front of the handle. Grandpa had explained how the machine guns worked, although he had not let Tommy use them. Maybe one day, Tommy thought.

As the plane rolled right, he saw a field at the edge of Warrior Swamp's green blanket of treetops. His attention seemed drawn to the area: It was flat, though not plowed. It looks like a runway, Tommy thought. The field slipped out of sight. Tommy focused again on flying.

Ten minutes later, the Warhawk descended toward

Grandpa's barn. Once on the ground, only part of the plane could be seen above the corn. The plants had grown to more than seven feet tall and were gradually turning from green and silky to tan and brittle. Long ears of corn wrapped in leafy husks poked out from the stalks.

"Landing is one of the next big things we'll need to work on," Grandpa said as he taxied toward the barn. "You're ready to try it, though. You have been an excellent student."

The praise warmed Tommy. He and Grandpa had been flying for weeks. Tommy had not flown by himself. Yet he had grown comfortable with piloting the plane under his grandfather's coaching. He had even practiced takeoffs. Grandpa told him the biggest problem with takeoffs in the powerful P-40 was keeping "the back end from outrunning the front."

After supper one night, Tommy overheard Grandpa tell his mom he considered Tommy a natural.

Tommy was not sure what that meant, but he liked the sound of it.

Flying fascinated him. What had once seemed a maze of gauges and switches and knobs now made sense. The feel of the plane in flight was comfortable, not scary. Even the few bumps and dips in flight were familiar. Grandpa had explained how air acted something like water, with turbulence mirroring invisible currents and the movement of the air along the landscape below.

Tommy also liked studying about the P-40. He stayed up late at night memorizing the flight manual at Grandpa's kitchen table. Sam helped sometimes, using the manual to quiz Tommy about cockpit controls and flying situations.

Sam liked flying, too. However, he seemed more interested in how the plane and its parts worked. He had quickly discovered that the radio in the P-40 could sometimes pick up the same channels he monitored with his father's radio. Sam once contacted his brother Ben while in the air.

Tommy noticed that Sam's concern about his brother and what Ben might be facing had grown. As summer slipped into what Grandpa called dog days, a season of stifling heat and humidity eased only by an occasional evening thunderstorm, Sam often seemed preoccupied or worried. He also spent more time listening to the CB radio in his father's pickup truck.

Tommy wanted to help Sam. He just was not sure how.

After the morning's flight lesson, Tommy and Grandpa ate a late lunch of leftover spaghetti. Tommy's mother was spending the day packing with his dad at their home. For Tommy and Grandpa that meant they could clean up later. "We'll get to the table sometime before bedtime," Grandpa said. He switched on the radio and found the Atlanta Braves in the first inning of an afternoon game with the Philadelphia Phillies.

Grandpa headed toward his rocking chair. "Tommy, we'll take it easy for an hour or two before we go back ..."

The phone rang.

"Must be your mom and dad," Grandpa said as he reached for the receiver.

His expression after saying hello showed Tommy it was not his parents.

Grandpa started to speak. He frowned instead. His jaw clenched and his cheeks reddened. Suddenly he barked, "No!" and slammed the receiver into the phone cradle.

Grandpa wheeled and strode out of the house. Tommy heard him mutter, "Last chance, my foot!"

The kitchen door slammed shut behind him.

✪ Chapter 10 ✪

Get the Plane!

G randpa was hoeing at the hottest time of the afternoon. The hoe blade flashed in the sun as he chopped at bahiagrass grass clinging beside bushy rows of beans. He was wearing a wide-brimmed straw hat, and a stain of sweat grew dark and wide along the band of the hat.

Sam arrived red-faced on his bicycle minutes after Tommy telephoned him. "What's up?" he panted.

Tommy told him about the telephone call. "Grandpa is trying to cool down."

Sam peered out the window. "Doesn't look like it. So you think the call was from Sunglasses?"

Sunglasses is the name Sam and Tommy had given the man who visited months before, wearing black sunglasses and wanting to buy the Warhawk.

"I don't know who else it could have been," Tommy said. "I just wonder what might happen next. Grandpa has said he didn't think they would try to steal the plane. But he wasn't sure."

Sam thought for a minute. "We need a plan."

They decided to spend that night in Tommy's room. Grandpa would not mind. They could secretly take turns staying awake and watching out the bedroom windows for Sunglasses. "And whoever else he brings," Sam said.

"Whomever," Tommy corrected.

"Huh?" said Sam.

"'Whomever' is right. Not 'whoever,'" Tommy said.

"Nobody knows that," Sam grumbled. "Nobody cares, either."

The plan seemed a good one; except that Sunglasses came that afternoon, not that night. Tommy and Sam were beside the backyard shed, arguing over who would stand watch after midnight, when they saw a black car move slowly up the dirt road and turn into Grandpa's driveway. The boys dived behind the shed and peeked around the corner.

A thin man in a white polo shirt and blue jeans got out of the driver's side. He scanned the yard. The front door on the passenger side opened. Tommy felt his stomach sink. It was Sunglasses. Tommy could not forget the tan face, slick black hair and dark sunglasses.

The men walked to the carport and out of the boys' view.

Tommy leaned against the shed. Sam was still looking. "Your grandpa went inside the house earlier, right?" he whispered.

Tommy nodded. His mind raced. What should he do? What could he do?

An idea came. He suddenly knew. He was afraid, though.

"Sam," Tommy said, his voice shaking, "you've got to go for help. I don't know what's going on. They could just be trying to talk Grandpa into selling. But I don't think so. I'm worried."

"What are you going to do?" Sam asked.

"I've got to see if I can help Grandpa here."

"But ..." Sam started.

"No," Tommy interrupted. "You've got to get your dad or call Ben or somebody! Now hurry. Please!"

Sam looked at his friend. "OK. I'll leave my bike here and cut through the corn. If I try the road, they might spot me. But I'll be fast!"

Sam turned and ran to the corn. At the edge of the field he looked back, then darted into the opening between two rows and disappeared in the dense plants.

Tommy glanced at the sky. It had turned from blue-white to bronze. He and Grandpa should be up there flying, he thought. He took a deep breath and looked around the corner of the shed. No one else was outside. The summer afternoon lay still. Tommy heard only the hum of gnats around his face, and the pulse pounding in his ears.

He crouched and sprinted toward the house.

Tommy ran to the back wall and huddled against it, pressing into the rough bricks. He caught his breath before easing along the wall to a living room window. Sweat trickled down his face. He could hear the muffled sounds of people talking inside. Tommy rose slowly until he could see over the window ledge and into the room.

Grandpa was sitting in a chair in the far corner. His arms and hands were behind the chair. He looked stiff and angry. The man in the white shirt stood in the opposite corner with his arms folded. Sunglasses was walking back and forth in front of Grandpa. Tommy sucked in his breath when he saw what Sunglasses was holding: a black pistol. It looked big, even in his chunky hand.

"Where's the boy?" Sunglasses asked gruffly.

"Home with his parents. I already told you," Grandpa said.

"I'm not sure I believe you. But it doesn't matter. In a short while, we will be gone."

"You just can't walk away with an airplane," Grandpa said.

"Walk?" Sunglasses laughed. "Oh, Mr. Tillman, we are not going to walk. We are going to fly. At least, one of us is."

He waved the gun toward the other man. "Captain here is good at making special planes disappear."

"The Bible has a word for you both," Grandpa said. "I'll give you a hint: It starts with 'f' and rhymes with 'tools.'"

Tommy smiled as he whispered to himself, "Fools!"

Sunglasses was not smiling. "Mr. Tillman, I was willing to pay you a handsome price for your plane. Now, I will get it for nothing. And I'm the fool?"

Sunglasses turned to Captain. "Go get the plane!"

Captain left the room.

The command had a stronger effect on Tommy. He bolted for the path. He knew he had to get to the barn before Captain. What he would do then was not clear.

He ran down the path, rounding the curve between the house and barn, hoping he made it before Captain spotted him. His tennis shoes dug into the soft sand. The path had never seemed so long.

Tommy was sweating when he reached the barn. He fumbled under the loose board where Grandpa kept an extra key. His fingers touched metal. Breathing hard, he grabbed the key. His hands trembled as he unlocked the door and pushed it open.

A barrage of sound hit him. A blaring "WOO-AAA, WOO-AAA" hammered his senses. The alarm! He had forgotten that Grandpa kept the alarm set!

Tommy rushed to the switch by the door. He flicked it off. The alarm did not stop. He flipped the switch back; no change. Tommy rapidly clicked the switch up, down, up, down, but the horn did not stop.

He slammed his hand against the wall. The sound filled his ears. Captain would be here any second. He had to get the P-40 away!

Tommy ran for the roll-back doors. Tears of frustration

welled up in his eyes. He could not think clearly. He would never be able to get the plane out in time. This was too hard!

He angrily pushed open one of the doors.

Sam was standing there.

"Sam," Tommy yelled above the din, "you're supposed to be getting help!"

"Dad's not there!" Sam yelled back. "I couldn't reach Ben and I called the Sheriff's Office. I don't think they believed me."

Tommy's heart sank. "Sam, Captain's coming to get the Warhawk!"

"Captain?" Sam looked confused. The alarm's ringing ricocheted off the walls and concrete floor.

"You have to help me!" Tommy shouted.

"You want me to help you captain the Warhawk?"

Tommy could not know that triggering the alarm *had* helped him. At the house, Grandpa heard the sound and chuckled. "Well, I'll be," he said to himself. Sunglasses looked out the window and back at Grandpa. Captain hesitated in the back yard.

"That alarm can be heard halfway around the county," Grandpa said. "We will have some company here before long."

"Quiet!" Sunglasses hissed. "Tillman, shut off the alarm. Now!"

✪ Chapter 11 ✪

The Only Way

T ommy and Sam had rolled the P-40 out of the barn when the alarm stopped. The silence seemed eerie.

"Get in," Tommy said.

"The plane?" Sam asked.

Tommy was already on the wing. He scrambled into the front of the cockpit. Sam followed, taking the back seat. Each put on a headset. They adjusted seat straps and clicked the buckles shut. Tommy began turning controls.

"Tommy," Sam said hesitantly, "is this the only way to save the Warhawk?"

"Yes," Tommy said, checking settings and switches.

"And you can do this?"

"Yes," Tommy said.

"Well, do it fast because somebody is coming."

Tommy looked back. The man Sunglasses called Captain was at the end of the barn path and jogging toward them. Tommy pushed the starter to engage the plane's engine.

"Please let it fire," he prayed. The P-40 thundered to life.

Captain slowed to a walk. He seemed unsure what to do. Tommy hurriedly adjusted fuel and propellor settings, scanned gauges and worked the wing flaps as he taxied the plane onto the edge of the runway. He turned the long nose down the stretch of grass and whispered to himself Grandpa's list of things to check before takeoff.

As if realizing what was happening, Captain started

running for the P-40. Tommy smoothly moved the throttle control forward. The plane began rolling, slowly at first, then faster.

Sam was watching Captain. The thin man had caught up to the plane and had one hand on the tail. As the Warhawk picked up speed, Captain held on. His arm stretched out farther until he was leaning nearly parallel to the ground. He either refused to let go or for some reason could not. The plane pulled him forward, his legs loping in longer and longer strides in a hopeless attempt to keep up.

Then Captain tripped. He fell, rolled in the dust and ended up on his knees, coughing and staring dazedly at the P-40 as it bellowed away.

Looking back, Sam grinned and gave him a thumbs-up.

In the front cockpit, Tommy struggled to keep the plane straight. He had handled takeoffs before. But that was with Grandpa in the back seat. The plane hurtled toward the corn at the end of the runway. Tommy glanced back and forth from gauges to the runway, sizing up the remaining distance. The P-40 surged forward. The corn was coming fast.

Then, with the feeling of exhilaration that always surprised him, the rattling ride down the runway turned instantly to smoothness as the plane became airborne. Tommy realized he had been holding his breath. He exhaled in relief. The plane wobbled slightly as it cleared the tasseled corn tops.

"Awesome!" Sam shouted.

Tommy smiled and wiped his face on his arm. He tried not to think beyond that moment, to when he would have to land.

"Can't steal what you can't catch!" he radioed.

He raised the landing gear, checked his airspeed indicator and other instruments, and steered the P-40 toward the house.

"Look!" Sam cried. "On the road below your granddad's!"

Tommy dipped the left wing and spotted a gold-colored

patrol car speeding toward the house. Clouds of dust trailed it. The light on its roof winked blue. Farther behind, Tommy saw another patrol car with its light flashing. He laughed. Help was on the way! Sam's telephone call had done the job.

Then he saw Sunglasses. The man appeared beside Grandpa's carport far below. He looked toward the road and up at the P-40 and walked quickly to the black car. Captain was there, too, running across the back yard.

Almost without thinking, Tommy pushed the control stick forward. The Warhawk dropped toward the house.

The rising howl of the descending plane caused Captain to look up. The P-40 bore down on him. The late-afternoon sun glinted on the snarling mouth. Captain's mouth opened wide in surprise.

He turned, tripped and fell again.

Sunglasses had the car door open. He screamed when he saw the plane, spun around and dove for the front seat. However, the door frame was lower than he thought. The big man slammed head-first into the metal. He crumpled to the ground. Cracked sunglasses dangled from one ear.

The P-40 rumbled overhead.

"Oh, man!" Tommy said. "Did you see what Sunglasses did when he saw us?"

"Unbelievable!" Sam cheered.

Tommy nosed the plane up, gaining altitude. As he did, it struck him that he was flying the P-40 by himself. With no one helping!

To the west, he glimpsed clumps of blue and purple clouds, signs of a storm brewing. Circling over the house, he saw the patrol cars slide into Grandpa's yard. Deputies jumped out. Captain raised his hands. Sunglasses did not move. From the air, he looked like a rumpled heap of clothes.

And there was Grandpa! He was walking out from under

the carport. He was looking up and waving!

"Sam, Grandpa's OK! Do you see him?" Tommy radioed.

There was only silence. Tommy twisted in his seat to see his friend. Sam's face was pale.

"I was checking the radio to see if I could reach Ben," Sam said. "I believe I heard him.

"He's calling for help."

❂ Chapter 12 ❂

Ben

S witching his headset to receive the same radio signal, Tommy first heard only static. Through the crackling, he made out Ben's voice.

"10-33! 10-33! Do you read me? Officer fired on at the edge of Warrior Swamp! West of Bender and Simon roads. I'm pinned down. On a runway by the swamp ..."

Popping noises interrupted Ben. The static closed back in, drowning out the rest of his call.

Tommy felt stunned. The frantic plea rang in his ears. He circled the house, his hand on the control stick and his feet on the rudder pedals moving automatically. One of the patrol cars below spun around in Grandpa's front yard. Sand spewed from its tires. The car fish-tailed onto the road and accelerated. Its blue light had never stopped flashing.

Sam spoke. "10-33 is code for an emergency. Ben is in trouble. I think those were gun shots at the end of the call."

Tommy tried to think through what his friend was saying. Something nagged at him. Something in what Ben had said about Warrior Swamp and a runway. Something Tommy could not quite remember. Or, maybe he could.

"Sam!" Tommy shouted. "I think I know where Ben is!"

He turned the plane west and pushed the throttle forward. Power surged through the P-40, pressing both boys back against their seats. Tommy watched the gauges tracking speed and revolutions per minute swing upward. Miles ahead, a black-green band marked the border of Warrior Swamp. The forest looked even darker against the thunderstorm building on the horizon beyond it.

"Grandpa and I were flying over the swamp this morning," Tommy said. "I saw a cleared field at one edge. I didn't know what it was. But I think it might have been the runway Ben is talking about!"

"I hope you're right," Sam said. His voice sounded small.

Tommy understood. He hoped he was right, too. If so, they would get there before the deputies. Then, Tommy thought, the question would be the same they had faced earlier: What could they do?

The immediate answer seemed to him the only thing to do. He began to pray silently.

"Tommy! Listen!" Sam had picked up a conversation on the radio. It was a different person, yet still one that Tommy had heard before.

"This is Yellow Dog coming home," a man said. "Is supper ready?"

The reply followed a long silence. "Hold off, Yellow Dog," another voice commanded. "Landing strip is occupied."

"Occupied? ... OK. Over."

Sam interrupted: "I think that was the pilot in the drugs plane talking to the people on the ground. They must have told him not to land because Ben is there."

Sam paused. "How long before we get there?"

"Maybe five minutes," Tommy said.

He sounded more confident than he felt. He kept glancing out each side of the cockpit, trying to retrace the route he and Grandpa had flown that morning that took them over the odd-looking field, the one he hoped was a runway.

Nothing looked the same now.

Tommy flew due west. The storm loomed ahead, filling the view in front of the cockpit and blocking the evening sun. Where is that place? Tommy wondered.

Sam spotted the runway first. "There it is! On the right!"

Tommy whispered, "Thank you!" and banked the plane toward what looked like a grass landing strip between thick forest and a field of soybeans. As the P-40 drew closer, Tommy's stomach grew hollow at what he saw.

Ben's truck was at one end of the runway. A green pickup truck and a red car were parked 50 yards away. Two men crouched behind the car and three behind the truck. Some aimed what looked like rifles or shotguns. Tommy saw smoke spit from the barrels. They were firing at Ben.

Sam's brother huddled behind the front of his pickup. He would rise, shoot what Tommy guessed was a pistol and drop behind the truck again.

Ben looked up as the P-40 flew past. In that instant, his truck windshield exploded in a spray of glass.

✪ Chapter 13 ✪

Attack

"We have to help!" Sam sounded scared.

Tommy swung the P-40 over the swamp. His thoughts were scattered, like a jumble of jigsaw puzzle pieces. There were no patrol cars in sight. Flying low over the field might not help. The people shooting at Ben might shoot at the Warhawk. "But Ben will get hurt or worse if I don't do something," Tommy said to himself.

He turned back toward the field. The angle of flight would bring the plane behind the two vehicles that flanked Ben's truck. Tommy made his decision, picked out the red car and tilted the plane's nose down.

He reached forward and flicked switches. The P-40 sloped toward the car. Tommy straightened in his seat and adjusted the descent to line up the car in the gun sight. He whispered, "Grandpa, I know I don't have your permission, but I hope you'll forgive me."

Sam heard the last half of Tommy's confession. "Forgive you for what?" he asked.

Instead of answering, Tommy squeezed the trigger on the control stick. The six machine guns in the wings rattled. Remembering what he had read in the pilot's manual, Tommy counted off the seconds aloud – "one, two, three" – and released the trigger.

On the runway, the men using the car as a shield had watched the P-40 circle and return. They stared without moving as the plane approached. Then they heard the *brrraaaaaappttt* of its machine guns. Tracers trailing white smoke whipped toward them.

One man started to shoot back, thought better of it and jumped behind the car. The other man tried to squeeze under the car as a hail of 3-inch-long bullets slammed into the field nearby, flinging dirt head-high.

"That's great!" yelled Sam, looking down as the P-40 roared past. "Let's get the others!"

Tommy was already concentrating on clearing the trees and pulling around for another pass. The three men at the truck squatted beside it. They had seen what happened. As the P-40 slid toward them, Tommy could see all three aiming at the plane. Their guns flashed.

Tommy tried to concentrate on centering the truck in the ring-and-dot sight. These men were more prepared for his attack. But so was he.

Sand flew as the P-40's guns stitched six lines of small explosions that raced toward the truck and tore through it. Fist-sized holes appeared in the sides. The men scattered. As Tommy pulled up, bright light flashed below. The P-40 shook. A dull *whomp* cut through the throaty grumbling of the plane's engine.

Sam was yelling again. "It blew up, Tommy! The truck just blew up!"

Tommy could see it now. The cab and bed of the green pickup had been ripped apart. Blackened metal twisted up and out from the frame. Smoke poured from the front. Pieces of tire smoldered in the grass. Tommy wanted to say "Wow" but no sound came out.

As the P-40 rose, he saw sheriff's patrol cars – three, four, even more – racing along a dirt road a half-mile away. Sam was watching the drug runners. They were trying to escape.

"They're running scared!" Sam said.

The red car bounced across the runway, stopping to pick up the men from the destroyed truck. Ben jumped in his truck, peering through the blown-out windshield. The deputies in the patrol cars had discovered the lane that led to the runway. Their cars streamed down it.

Sam tried to tune in the police radio channel, hoping to hear the chase. Tommy saw Ben's truck skid to a stop. The door flung open. Ben leaned out and stared up at the P-40. Then he waved his arms and pointed at them, jabbing his finger at the sky.

Sam saw his brother, too. "He looks worried."

"Is he pointing at us?" Tommy asked. "Or above us?"

He glanced through the top of the cockpit and stopped talking. He was shocked to see that the storm had almost reached them. Swollen, gray clouds towered overhead. Gusts of wind rocked the plane. Tommy had been too occupied to notice them before.

Was Ben trying to warn them about the storm? he wondered.

Wham! Something struck the cockpit canopy like a hammer blow. Tommy and Sam ducked instinctively. Tommy looked up to see the glass fractured into a spider web-like pattern near his head. "What was that?" he said.

A yellow plane pulled alongside the P-40. The plane looked like a two-seat crop duster. It had low wings and a cockpit set high on the fuselage. The back half of the cockpit was open. Sitting inside it, a man struggled to steady a long black rifle. It was pointed at Tommy and Sam.

❂ Chapter 14 ❂

Yellow Dog

The next shot missed as Tommy peeled the P-40 away from the crop duster and into a dive. Tommy waited until he was 1,000 feet above the ground to level out. The dive put the fighter plane a safe distance from the yellow plane. Tommy knew, though, that any good crop-duster pilot would have no trouble following him.

Sam confirmed as much.

"He's still on our tail, Tommy. Just behind and above us."

"That has to be Yellow Dog," Sam added.

Tommy felt a chill run through him. He checked his instruments. The fuel gauge was edging toward empty. The dive had sent him away from Grandpa's farm. He could outrun the crop duster, try to cut around him and run for home. Or ...

A sharp crack and a simultaneous metallic clang cut short his thoughts. Tommy spotted a long gash in the right wing. Yellow Dog had caught up with the P-40 and the attacker's third shot had hit its mark. The man in the back seat of the crop duster was aiming again.

Tommy felt his anger rise. This was his grandfather's plane. Not Sunglasses'. Not Captain's. And certainly not some drug dealer's.

"We can run," Tommy muttered to himself, "or we can fight."

He pushed the P-40 to full throttle. The speeding fighter

quickly left the crop duster trailing behind. The two planes soared over Warrior Swamp. Trees, creeks and cane thickets rushed beneath. The radio issued a dull hum. The swamp was a dead zone for radio transmissions. Tommy and Sam were on their own.

"Tommy," Sam asked, "are we trying to get away?"

"Not for long," Tommy answered.

"I'm with you," Sam said.

Tommy looked over his shoulder. "I don't know if everybody knew that," he said with a grin, "but I did."

Tommy glanced back again to pinpoint the crop duster. It looked like a yellow dot behind them.

"Here we go, Sam," he said and banked the P-40 into a turn. He tried to hold the controls steady until just before the plane had reversed course. Tommy drifted into the last of the 180-degree turn. The Warhawk was now flying straight at Yellow Dog.

As the planes sped toward each other, Tommy gripped the control stick tighter and tensed his legs and feet. He had read how one World War II P-40 pilot attacked Japanese planes head on. The machine guns on the P-40 had a longer range than the enemy's, something Grandpa had also told him. The advantage often prompted an opposing pilot to turn or dive away. That sometimes gave the Warhawk pilot a clear shot.

Now, with a different enemy and in a different fight, Tommy hoped Yellow Dog would do the same.

The two planes were closing at faster than 350 mph. Tommy saw the crop duster grow bigger and bigger. His hand clenched the control stick.

Abruptly, Yellow Dog veered left. He also slowed. The maneuver should have caused the P-40 to zip past the smaller plane, giving its gunman another shot.

Instead, when Yellow Dog turned, Tommy swerved in the

same direction. Rapidly overtaking the other plane, he saw it fill his gun sight for a split-second. He had time for only a burst of machine-gun fire. But as the Warhawk zoomed up and over the crop duster, Tommy saw tracer bullets smack the yellow plane's belly, scattering sparks. Shards of yellow metal fluttered like feathers in midair.

"You hit him, Tommy!" Sam said. "He's going down! Yessss!"

The crop duster spewed smoke as it sank toward Warrior Swamp. Tommy circled to watch from above. Yellow Dog obviously knew about the runway along the swamp. He flew straight for it, barely clearing the forest edge and landing hard on the grass. The plane rolled to a halt. Patrol cars surrounded it.

"That's more sheriff's cars than I have ever seen in one place," Sam said.

As Tommy started to reply a gust of wind pushed the Warhawk sideways and pelted it with rain. Lightning gashed the dark sky. The storm had come. Time to stop gawking and start moving, Tommy decided.

"Sam, we are going to have to run from this!" he said.

"Amen!" answered Sam.

Tommy turned the P-40 east toward Grandpa's. With the storm at their backs, he and Sam raced for home, talking and laughing about Yellow Dog, the blown-up truck and Sunglasses. As they talked Tommy tried not to think about what lay ahead.

Not yet.

✪ Chapter 15 ✪

Into the Storm

The changing network of fields and roads showed Tommy they were nearing home. The thunderstorm followed close behind. The P-40 was low on fuel. Yet with the storm winds pushing the plane forward, Tommy knew his challenge would not be conserving fuel – it would be getting on the ground, and before the brunt of the storm struck.

He rehearsed in his mind what he had heard Grandpa recite before landings. Landing gear down. Flaps down. Nose up. Trim to glide. Make sure your safety belt is fastened.

Tommy had never landed the P-40. He had not even tried with Grandpa helping him. Now he had to do it alone.

Tommy smiled grimly as he recalled Grandpa's description of working the rudder pedals during a landing. He said fighter pilots called it the dance of death.

Grandpa's house and the runway came into view. The runway ran east-west through the cornfield. Tommy figured that the storm blowing east was an advantage. Landing into the wind would help slow the plane and provide extra lift under the wings.

Tommy flew past the runway and turned. The plane bucked as a heavy wind hit it broadside. Slightly shaken, Tommy decided it was time Sam knew.

"Sam," he said, "I have never landed a plane before."

"You've never what!"

"I have never landed a plane."

"This plane?" Sam asked.

"Any plane," Tommy replied.

Sam was thinking. "Where are the parachutes?" he asked.

Tommy giggled. He did not know how to bail out, either. Not that there were any parachutes.

"There aren't any," he said, giggling harder. "Everybody knows that."

He heard Sam laughing, too. The tension lifted.

"Oh, well," Sam said, catching his breath. "You land. I'll pray."

Tommy smiled. He had the P-40 in line with the green strip of grass. He was watching his gauges track the descent when movement on the ground drew his attention. People were running for the landing strip. One was Grandpa. And there were his mom and dad! And Sam's father was speeding along the barn path in his pickup, plowing over corn stalks as he cut across the curves.

The sight should have cheered the boys. Instead it made them both homesick. The lightness in the cockpit disappeared. Tommy knew that only a quarter-mile of air separated him and Sam from the people who loved them. It might as well be 100 miles, Tommy thought bitterly.

He had no idea what speed he needed to land, or the angle of approach, or exactly where or how to set the P-40 down. He was also tired. An hour of flying, of wrestling with the plane and thinking through a thousand things to stay in the air, had sapped his strength. A feeling of helplessness washed over him.

The storm rocked the P-40 again. "I've got to focus," Tommy told himself.

The full force of the storm had arrived. Rain lashed the cockpit. The wind howled, shoving the P-40 off course, sometimes forcing it downward. Tommy struggled to keep the wings level and the nose pointed toward the runway, now partially hidden by gray sheets of rain.

The plane was descending into a chaos that threatened to tear it from the sky.

"Tommy!" It was his father on the radio!

"Tommy, can you hear me?"

"Yes, Dad!" Tommy said, relieved. Sam must have been able to dial in his father's CB radio channel!

"Here's Grandpa," Tommy's father said, talking fast. "Do what he says. We love you."

Grandpa spoke next.

"Tommy, pull back up. Now! You're coming in too high."

"I ..." Tommy started.

"Do it," Grandpa ordered. "Circle the runway. Keep it steady. The Warhawk can handle this storm. So can you."

Tommy followed his grandfather's instructions. The P-40 bounced and shuddered. But Tommy soon had the plane set for a second landing attempt. Grandpa talked him through the approach.

The P-40 angled down, swaying and wallowing in the wind. Even with Grandpa's instructions, Tommy had the sickening feeling that the runway was rising more rapidly than it should. The plane plunged through the swirling rain toward the field.

Something is not right! Tommy thought. Fear gripped him. This is too fast!

He braced for the impact. "Hold on, Sam!"

The Warhawk's wheels touched. The plane bounced. A gust slammed it back down. The left wing dipped, slicing the tip into the ground. The plane began spinning.

The P-40 whirled across the grass. The force pinned

Tommy and Sam against the side of the cockpit. Tommy glimpsed brown-green corn rushing at them. Wet plants clattered against the plane, slapping and snapping. Mud and pieces of leaves spattered the canopy. Metal groaned. The engine rose to an ear-splitting whine. Then it died.

The spinning slowed. As if weary, the plane sloshed to a stop, tilted onto one wheel, balanced for a second and fell back to the earth with a clump.

Tommy sat in shock. Rain, falling softer as the storm passed, drummed on the canopy. He stared upward, his body jammed into the side of the plane. His eyes absently traced drops trickling along the outside of the glass. He could smell the sick-sweet scent of fuel and burnt oil. The smells and the rain seemed far off.

Footsteps thumped on the wing. A face appeared, stared at Tommy and smiled. The canopy rolled back. Cool, wet air flowed in. People talked excitedly. Strong arms lifted him out. He was trembling. He turned and saw Sam.

Sam was pale but grinning.

The shock began to clear. Tommy's parents were hugging him, laughing and crying. Warmth spread through him.

He was home. He and Sam had made it home.

✪ Chapter 16 ✪

Everybody Knows

B reakfast the next morning came late and lasted longer than usual. Sam and his parents joined Tommy's family at Grandpa's house. Between bites of biscuits and scrambled eggs, Tommy and Sam told every detail they could recall – and some they weren't sure about but thought might have happened – from the time they saw Sunglasses and Captain arrive until they landed the Warhawk.

Ben stopped by while they were eating. He said Yellow Dog and his companions were in jail, and court hearings had been scheduled. No, Yellow Dog did not work at the grocery store in town. That was only rumor, Ben explained.

The pilot was from Florida, but he knew people in the area, including the landowner who had cleared the runway beside Warrior Swamp.

"He is being charged, too," Ben said of the runway's owner.

Sunglasses and Captain were sharing a jail cell, he said. Sunglasses was an Atlanta businessman who collected historic warplanes, apparently sometimes illegally. Captain had once flown for a major airline. Investigators were still determining his connection to Sunglasses.

The investigators would also need to talk to Sam and Tommy after lunch, Ben said.

Before leaving, he patted Sam on the back. "I have to say that I have never been more surprised or glad to see that green plane with the shark's mouth. Even if it was my newest neighbor and my little brother in the cockpit!"

Tommy's father agreed. "We are all glad and very grateful for how everything turned out."

He nodded at Grandpa. "Did you tell the boys about their ammunition?"

"What about the ammo?" Tommy asked, still chewing a piece of biscuit.

Grandpa sipped his coffee. "You didn't have enough left to spit at," he said. "The box for each gun holds about 230 rounds, enough for 10 seconds of firing. You used all but the last few rounds. If you hadn't hit Yellow Dog when you did, you might have really been forced to run for it!"

As others laughed, Tommy thought for a minute, staring at his plate. "Grandpa, I know you didn't give me permission to use the guns."

"No, but in this case" said Grandpa, winking at Tommy's mother and father, "I'm not going to ground you."

Tommy looked up. "How is the Warhawk? That's why we took off in it. I didn't want Sunglasses to get it."

"It'll be OK," Grandpa said. "There are plenty of repairs to make, but nothing I haven't done before. Of course, the last time I did them was 30 years ago."

After breakfast, Grandpa, Tommy and Sam walked to the barn to see the plane. A mockingbird sang from the peak of the tin roof. Sunshine lit the interior of the barn through the rolled-back doors. The storm had washed the sky dazzling blue. The air was cool, a welcome sign that before long summer would fade into fall.

"Grandpa, what would have happened if I had tried to land on that first approach?" Tommy asked.

"You two would have ended up in the neighbor's field. If you made it through the fencerow and the trees," he said.

Tommy noticed a gash in the wing. He thought of the gunman shooting at them. "How did we do it?" he said, thinking aloud.

"What's that?" asked Grandpa.

Tommy shook his head. "I was just asking myself, I guess, how we did it. How we flew the plane, how we helped rescue Ben and all that. It feels like something that happened to somebody else. Not me and Sam. We're not even teenagers yet!"

Grandpa studied his grandson. The boy appeared older, as if he had grown.

"You did it by skill, yours and Sam's," Grandpa said. "And because you have a God who listens to the prayers of parents and granddads and boys."

Tommy remembered when he first saw the P-40. It had amazed him then. It still did. He touched the painted mouth on the fuselage. "Will you ever sell it?" he asked.

Grandpa put a hand on Tommy's shoulder. "Sell? Maybe that time will come. For now, it's time to patch up this warbird and get it back in the air.

"After all, I have a couple of true Flying Tigers in my crew!"

Sam and Tommy smiled at each other.

"Of course," said Grandpa, glancing at Sam, "everybody knows that."

About the Author

Rick Lavender grew up in Florida and south Georgia. He graduated from Mercer University and earned a master's degree in journalism from the University of Georgia.

Rick worked as a writer and editor with Georgia newspapers and outdoors magazines for more than 25 years, including 18 years with The Times in Gainesville. He now works in public relations with the Georgia Department of Natural Resources.

He and his wife and children live in Watkinsville, Georgia.

Made in the USA
Charleston, SC
12 November 2012